Chapter & Verse

Chapter & Verse

R.T. Walton

Chapter & Verse

R.T. Walton

Published by Aspect Design 2013
Malvern, Worcestershire, United Kingdom.

Designed, printed and bound by Aspect Design
89 Newtown Road, Malvern, Worcs. WR14 1PD
United Kingdom
Tel: 01684 561567
E-mail: allan@aspect-design.net
Website: www.aspect-design.net

Cover Design Copyright © 2013 Aspect Design
Original photograph Copyright © 2013
ISBN 978-1-908832-40-5

CONTENTS

FOREWORD

By way of an introduction to the stories and the poems in this book, much of the content was unlocked after undergoing a period of counselling as a result of reading M. Scott Peck's *The Road Less Travelled* nearly three decades ago. The poem *Alchemy* was written as a tribute and in thanks to Easton Hamilton of *The Reach Approach* after my immersion into the rich dark waters of psychotherapy.

The Empty Window and *Sky Bird* were stories born from hours spent in the classroom as a teaching assistant, undertaking many of the tasks set during lesson time. *The Girl Who Gave Everything Away*, an attempt to protect one of my pupils, intent on running a reckless course. Taking care to use words familiar to my student, and the formula of repetition, hoped to discretely impart its warning by giving her the story as 'reading practice'.

The short two to three line poems were my attempt at *Haiku* and though I might have been able to assemble my thoughts into seventeen syllables for the most part, am grateful for the feedback from an associate editor at *Heron's Nest* a quarterly on-line journal. Nevertheless, I fondly include them here anyway, as mindscapes and meditations, and hope you enjoy reading them as I did composing them.

Finally, my thanks to Christopher Baker, Easton Hamilton and Vincent Claridge for their encouragement and support in this project and for their loving friendship over the years.

R.T.W.
2013

By the time one realizes there are
but a finite number of opportunities,
the simplest act of kindness becomes
something akin to devotion.

For Christopher.

Part 1

Chapter

GREENHEART AND THE GIANT

Not too long ago and not too far away, in the foothills of the Great Mountain, there lived a giant. At the other end of the valley, in a small hamlet just around the bend in the river, lived the people of Satya, their friendly houses clustered together in comfortable companionship.

About them lay fields and orchards, yielding and lush in their grains and fruits. And so the people of Satya lived happily and gently, dancing with the seasons, accepting with joy what nature, in her own time provided.

But life was not so for the giant, where the barren and rocky land was swept by arid winds and burned by cruel frosts, so that no vegetation clothed the naked body of the earth. At night the giant took shelter in a cave. By day he roamed the rocky wilderness searching for insects and small creatures and they were *his* sustenance.

Now, as is customary among the good people of Satya, every child is named in the fifth year of life at the Choosing ceremony. And so it was for Greenheart, who as the Choosing implies, was bestowed this most fitting name in celebration and in thanks for a particularly good harvest.

At the end of the sixth year, when Greenheart had seen yet another full four seasons, the Choosing was still in place. And indeed, it seemed as though Greenheart had been born *with* the name and that the Choosing and the Child were one.

❧❧❧

Late one day in the mid-point of the year, little Greenheart was returning home and having still some way to go, took the westward route into the setting sun and soon entered a strange and barren valley high up among the foothills of the Great Mountain. Little Greenheart knew nothing of the giant but the giant *knew* that someone had entered his valley.

For half an afternoon the giant had watched the tiny figure's descent into the valley and now he could see it was a little child. All the while the giant brooded and scowled, jealous of his isolation, his brain filled with half formed plans of abduction and murder. The longer the giant watched the child, the greater grew his rage at the violation of his wilderness and now the giant spoke, his voice brittle with disuse and rasping with hatred, 'Who comes to trespass?'

'It is I, Greenheart' replied the child and a thousand ice bells softly tinkled.

'What business have you here?' roared the giant.

'I carry the seeds of Love in my heart' the child made reply and the wind took the word love in its warm embrace and carried it here and there.

The giant seized Greenheart by the shoulders, '*LOVE?*' he choked and spittle flecked his chin. 'I'll pluck out your *heart* before love comes to my lands'.

But the child did not flinch and held the giant's eyes without a flicker.

'Although you could not know *when*, you have *always* known that I would come. What would you have me do?' asked the child.

'*Do?*' spat the giant, '*DO?*' I'll tell you what I'd have you *do*' he mocked. 'I would have you bring me the bitter fruit of hatred and the sticky fruit of sweet revenge and I would have you bring me the spiny fruit of the counterfeit crab apple. Bring me these three fruits or I will surely kill you!'

Each time the giant named the fruit, he shook the child and each time there was the sound as of a thousand petals softly falling.

'For the sake of Love I will return in three days' said the chid and was gone, even though the giant did not recollect loosening his fierce grip.

All the long day and the next, the giant waited for the child's return and the valley was cloaked in silence and a gloom descended and for the first time, it seemed to the giant a most desolate place.

On the third day a pale sun broke through the clouds and a cold wind whipped up from the north, but by the noon point the day was brighter. The wind had shifted bringing warmer air and then at first, *oh so faintly*, carried on the breeze came the sounds of tiny, tinkling bells. At length the figure of the child could be seen approaching the barren valley.

As before the giant bellowed his challenge 'Who comes to trespass?'

'You *know* it is Greenheart' chided the child softly and there was the sound of laughter as though from a thousand tiny throats.

This put the giant into a murderous rage and he would have seized the child save that he could not quite see well enough to do so. The giant rubbed his eyes – all else he could *most* clearly see – the rocks, the earth, the small pile of bones that were the debris of his meal, yet when he looked directly at the child, the tiny figure seemed to slip from sight, to buzz, to vibrate, to shimmer with light. In frustration the giant beat the air with his fists.

Then placing his hands upon his gnarled knees and bending low, the giant glared straight into the face of the child and with a cunning leer, for he thought to know the answer already, said, 'What of the thing I asked of you? Where is the fruit of bitter hatred?'

The child gazed into the face of the giant, 'You have wrongly named the fruit, it is the pomegranate of love you seek.' And so saying, the child held out a fruit of palest yellow and blushing pink.

'And what of the second thing I asked?' sneered the giant 'Where is the fruit of sweet revenge?'

Again the child said, 'You have wrongly named the fruit. It is the soothing, healing papaya that you seek' and the child held out an oval fruit of vivid green.

'And what of the third thing I asked? Where is the spiny counterfeit crab apple?' hissed the giant.

Once again the child said, 'You have wrongly named the fruit. It is the fragrant apple of wisdom that you seek' and the child held out an orb of deepest red and lush green.

A strange sound like a snarl and a sob exploded in the throat of the giant and he dashed the fruits from little Greenheart's outstretched hands and turning away, the giant strode some few paces and flung himself to the ground.

'I never should have let you enter my lands' grumbled the giant petulantly.

'It was *you* who called *me*' said Greenheart, 'or I never *could* have come.'

'I ought to kill you *now*.' said the giant savagely.

Oblivious to the giant's threat the child continued, 'And now there is something *you* must do. You must leave the valley and you must climb the mountain. That is all. I will see you by and by.' And so saying, the child grew brighter until there was only a patch of glowing air which spread and spread until it became too thin to see and the giant hurled a rock into the place where the child had stood.

For a long time the giant sat with his back against the boulder where he had flung himself and for the second time the valley of stone seemed a desolate and lonely place.

An icy wind whipped up around the stones and moaned about the crags and from the giant's right eye a single tear formed and was frozen on the instant. And the giant resolved that with the coming of a new day he should venture forth, for there was nothing for him here.

❧❧❧

Before the day's grey light had painted its drab monotone, the giant arose and stooping at the place where the fruits lay fallen, gathered them into his satchel of animal skins.

Now the giant greatly feared the mountain with its sheer rock walls and louring peak and he had never ventured into its stony ramparts. And yet it seemed that he should die of loneliness if he stayed, or perish on the perilous ascent if he should go, and although his step was faltering, he set his face toward the distant black cliffs not knowing how he should go, nor where he was bound, save that the rocky valley in whose confines he had dwelt so long had become an intolerable place.

❧❧❧

All day the giant walked in the grey light, until at evening he came to the foot of the Great Mountain and there being no visible way up the rock face, he sank to his knees. Just then, the giant felt he was not alone, and startled by the unseen presence, looked about him wildly.

'Who's there?' he cried dry lipped, 'Who's there I say!'

A thin emaciated figure of a man, old, stoop-shouldered and without a hair on his dome-like skull, was standing at the base of a vertical shaft of rock in the mountain. Clad only in a wretchedly thin coat of some lightish colour which flapped about him like a huge bird, revealing scrawny thighs, bony knees, large bare feet, blue with cold, the joints swollen and painful, the old man beckoned to the giant and without waiting, turned and began to climb the rock face by some small pathway that had been undetectable to the giant until now.

The giant followed, terrified of his decrepit guide, keeping as much distance between them as possible, yet not daring to lag behind for fear he should lose him altogether and be left to spend the coming night alone.

The path was steep and narrow and in places where the route turned tail and redoubled upwards, there was barely enough room on the rocky ledge to hold the giant's broad feet. Darkness came swiftly and the valley floor was mercifully blotted out in a depthless pool of inky black but the giant's imaginings took hold of him and threatened to topple him from the treacherous ledges even if his feet made not the error.

The old man was a pale spectre in the deepening murk and just when the giant felt his courage fail, the ancient guide stopped.

They were on a narrow mezzanine chamber in the rock and now the ancient figure turned to face the giant. And the old man spoke with a reedy voice.

'See this coat I wear? It is the garment of constraint. Many years ago I donned it proudly when it was a mantle of beliefs most cherished. But in my un-bending I forced others to wear this same coat and each time I cloaked another in my values, the wretched garment held *me* ever tighter in its grip.'

'It is a garment most unbecoming. I for one would not wear it', ventured the giant who had lost some of the terror he felt before the old man had started speaking.

The old man bowed his head.

'It is a common enough conceit I know, that a father wishes to mould a son in his own image and the cause of great bitterness between the two. Come, for I may go no further as your guide. Free me from this straitjacket and we can part as allies, for have I not delivered you safely thus far?'

The old man held out his arms and the giant gripped the coat in his hands and pulled and pulled and *pulled.*

The coat flailed and quivered like some hideous living skin and little by little the giant wrenched the thing from the old man's back and peeled the sleeves from the old man's spindly arms. All at once the loathsome garment was flapping free and with a shudder of disgust the giant hurled it away, where it sailed out over the edge of the rock. As it fell, it caught upon the air, spreading wide its folds like two leathery wings.

'It is done.' said the old man. 'Come you must refresh yourself and sleep for you have a long journey.'

Now the giant recollected that he had three fruits within the sling he carried and reaching inside, pulled one forth. In the darkness it was impossible to see which, but taking it between his large hands, the giant tore the fruit apart.

One half in each palm he made offering to the old man, who took and ate and the giant also. The fruit contained many pearls of sweet tasting juice which, as he ate, flooded his mouth with rose scented liquid, but each pearl also held a small bitter seed at its centre which lingered on his tongue long after the sweetness. And the giant was overcome with weariness and lying down upon the hard ground, he slept until dawn.

When the giant awoke, the old man was gone. He searched the narrow gallery to no avail but at the far end came upon a flight of steps, cut into the rock and with barely a pause he began to climb.

All through the day he climbed, quite alone, now and then glimpsing above him patches of sky between the gleaming black shafts of the mountain, but the precipice below swirled in mist and the valley floor was not visible.

All at once, at a turn in the stairway, stood a tall figure, hooded and cloaked and at the giant's approach it turned and proceeded before him and eventually they came to a rocky plateau high on the mountainside.

Again fear gripped the giant's heart, for the mysterious figure was terrifying to see, the face all hidden by the cowl it wore, but most terrifying was the eerie silence in which it stood.

Then the figure, raising its hands to its head, pulled back the hood and there, before the giant, stood a woman with silver hair. Still the woman did not speak but gazed upon the giant and with her right hand she pointed to a necklace strung with turquoise beads.

Again the woman raised her right hand in that same gesture, pointing at her throat. A band of precious stones encircled her neck in a grip that sought to choke her. A third time she pointed and entreated with her eyes in wordless plea and the giant knew what he must do.

So stepping forward he gripped the choker, and as he touched the stones, they burned white hot against his palm and he cried out in agony and tore his hand away with such force that the necklace broke and turquoise stones flew in every direction and landed on the ground about them, where they lay like liquid pools of pale blue acid.

And the woman let out a sigh that seared like hot sirocco and withered like arctic winds. At length she spoke.

'A mother's words can merely scold and chide the child, but if she is not careful, words grow in bitterness and condemnation and singe the delicate young wings of her fledgling child. Then words turning in upon the speaker who gives them utterance, smoulder deep within and blister the heart. But you have freed me. Come, do you have some healing salve within that bag you carry, for we are both in need of its cooling touch?'

The giant once more reached into the sling and brought out the second of the three fruits he had been given by little Greenheart. So ripe was the oval fruit that on striking it gently against the ground, it split in two, revealing soft, glistening, yellow-gold flesh which glowed in the dying light, and a seam of round black seeds gleamed like jet.

The woman and the giant shared the fruit and its flesh was soft and cooling, for it quieted the livid burn upon the giant's palm and doused the smouldering coals of scorn within the woman's breast and having eaten, the silver haired woman and the giant slept.

᭢᭢᭢

Now the giant passed his second night upon the mountain and on waking next morning, he was not surprised to find himself alone.

Once again the giant set his face toward the steep and rocky path that wound upwards and as before, he climbed all through the day until at last he came under the shadow of a great bluff at the mountain's summit. Here the giant thought to take some rest and he cast about him for a place among the boulders, when suddenly, his eye fell upon the crouching figure of a young woman.

The giant started and with a voice that shook called out 'Who are you and why do you fix me with such a look?'

The woman replied, 'Help me. I am lame.' and indeed the woman's foot was terribly afflicted, being turned inwards, so that she could not walk but drew herself along the ground.

'Help me,' she said again and raised her hand and the giant drew her up whereupon the woman wrapped her arms about the giant's neck in an embrace that was more pressing that the towering rocks, more stifling than an airless tomb, stronger than the serpent's coils about its prey.

The giant was afraid and cried out saying 'I do not know you woman, that you should clasp me thus. What do you *want*?'

The woman said 'You have the fragrant apple of wisdom in your bag. First let me eat.'

From his bag of skins the giant took the shining red-green orb and bit the apple in two. One piece he put into her mouth, the other he kept and ate and all the while the woman hung about his neck like lead. But when they had finished eating, the woman loosed her hold and unsupported stood before the giant.

Now the woman spoke. 'I have eaten of the fruit of wisdom. Hear me and my words shall set you free. I am she who shackles and keeps captive those who have bright visions of the future. I am she who fetters men's minds and stills his wonder. I am she who with counterfeit ways makes him fall into dull sleep and forget his dreams. See this crippled foot and know that my deeds have turned in upon the doer and fettered *me*.'

The day was drawing to a close and once again the giant made ready to pass his third night upon the mountain but the young woman said, 'Do *not* linger here. By attaining the summit this night you will fulfil *your* destiny and let me turn the course of mine.'

The giant who had also eaten of the apple of wisdom knew that the young woman spoke the truth.

In the dying light the giant heaved himself up the last few feet of the mountain, heedless of the rocks which grazed him, careless of the venomous creatures that dwelt in hole or crevice and into whose den he might unwittingly push his hands and feet. With the last of his strength and a terrible trembling in every limb, the giant laid himself upon the rocky summit, face up toward the sky and fell into an exhausted sleep.

⁂

Then the giant dreamed a strange and terrifying dream, that there did come a mountain storm, and thunder spoke above him with shock waves breaking over his body like a pounding sea. Jagged knives of lightning splintered the rocks beside him and now the giant felt his body start to shrink, growing smaller within the tattered garment fastened round his waist so that the folds of cloth threatened to stifle him like a dead man's shroud.

The pouch of animal skins slung about his shoulders became a living, breathing green eyed leopard, which snarling, sprang away from the body of the sleeping man. The strips of leather bound around his feet and legs began to writhe and in the vivid light of the storm, two huge serpents unwrapped themselves and fell away in gleaming coils to hide among the rocks. *And the giant had become a man.*

This was the dream.

⁂

Presently the coming dawn sent forth its airy messenger and a breeze sprang up about the mountain's sides, leaping from spar to spar until it found the man sleeping soft. It caressed his cheeks and playfully ruffled his hair and over his tunic, spun from finest wool, made ripples like soft desert sand. And the man awoke.

All about him the air was stained a deep and gentle pink, brightening from the east, spreading gold far up into the heavens, turning to palest yellow, through which the blue began to show. The man sat up and looked around in wonder and there on a rock a little way off was the child, playing with a rainbow.

The child slid from the rocky perch and alighted close to a patch of alpine flowers, then skipping delightedly around the tiny blossoms who nodded their translucent heads, little Greenheart laughed aloud for joy and said 'You have come at last!'

And the breeze took up the joyful welcome and sped down into the valley.

'And do you have the seeds of Love in your heart?' said the child.

'I do' the man replied, and his face was radiant.

Then taking the man's hand the child said 'Come then let us walk a while.'

HARI AND FATAKRI

Little Hari tumbled out of school along with the other children in Standard Three. Fifteen flying pairs of heels stirring up the smooth red-brown dust left the surface of the road pock marked with the imprint of small feet. Fifteen pairs of sharp little elbows flashed in the sunlight like pistons.

Hari didn't stop running until he rounded the bend in the dirt road that skirted the edge of the jungle. To the right lay wide water meadows, and beyond, the river. Hari lived in the small village which he could just see, now that he had come to the turn in the road. There in the distance, made watery in the heat haze, was his mother's house. From the small black rectangle that was the door, a tiny figure emerged into the fierce light and disappeared around the back.

Hari dragged his toes through the warm dust and began to loiter. He did this for two reasons. The first was that this was the place where his mongrel dog, Fatakri, usually greeted him and the second reason was that once home, his mother would set him to work, fetching firewood and helping his sister with other household chores. He would be kept busy until the evening meal was cooked and his father came home.

But on this day, Fatakri was not there to meet him, bounding up and throwing himself upon Hari gleefully, leaving powdery paw prints on his ragged cotton shirt – until Hari would repulse the dog with playful smacks. Then the dog would trot along in front of the boy until they reached the village.

Hari was puzzled by Fatakri's absence. He shifted his school slate from under one arm to the other and picked up a few stones, throwing them one by one. They landed with a dry plop on the dusty road.

As his eye followed the arc of each stone's flight, he noticed in the distance, some dark specks wheeling about in the sky further down the track. Carrion birds. Forgetting Fatakri, the boy started to run. As he got level, he saw a water buffalo. A large beast, lying on its side close to the road in the spiky grass at the edge of the field.

At his arrival several crows flapped upwards into the air, squawking their displeasure then grounded themselves almost at once, eyeing him sideways. The boldest crow hopped back onto the scrolled horn of the beast and cawed raucously. The buffalo was like a huge black tent that had fallen sideways, the ridgepole of its backbone parallel to the ground. One raised hip bone now formed the apex over which dark grey-black skin sloped away and this was why Hari did not immediately see Fatakri greedily feasting on the innards of the buffalo's split belly.

Fatakri was blissfully unaware of the arrival of his outraged young master. Whiskers red and sticky with gore, his jaws fastened upon a strip of gleaming pink flesh, Fatakri chewed and worried the carcass. His front legs were braced, paws splayed, head going from side to side, as he yanked at the dead buffalo. Slowly the fleshy ribbon came away with a wet, ripping sound.

Intent on eating the dead animal, Fatakri was taken unawares by his young master who was raining blows down upon the back of his velvety head. Surprised though unhurt and undeterred by the ferocity of the small boy's attack, he clamped his jaws deeper into the animal's viscera and from his mucous lined throat, emitted a deep, gurgling growl.

'*Haat sala*! Bad dog, dirty dog Fatakri!' Little Hari took hold of

Fatakri's golden brown scruff and tried to drag him off the buffalo. More in confusion than aggression, Fatakri continued to growl. With his small open hand Hari hit Fatakri squarely on the skull which made a hollow clunk. Fatakri blinked, let go and Hari fell backwards onto his bottom, one hand still clutching the pliable roll of fur and skin around the dog's neck.

The water buffalo now forgotten, Fatakri exuberantly greeted his young master Hari, shoving his wet nose into the boy's face, which for once was on the same level.

'*Chee*! Get away!' Hari slapped out and again crowned Fatakri. The dog stood there, head on one side, unsure if this was a new game. He tried wagging his tail to see.

Hari shouted again 'Dirty dog, how could you? *Chee*!' Hari jumped to his feet and made a grab for Fatakri and hauled him off across the field down to the river.

Only a short time later, had anyone used the dusty road that led to the village, at the place where the water meadows run down to the river, they might have seen death in the form of a motionless black buffalo and heard the ominous drone of attendant flies buzzing about the creature in dark spirals and clouds.

Or, they might have glanced out across the fields having heard the sound of a child's laughter and seen a small boy and a dog, happily splashing in the bright shallows. The boy standing waist high in the river, a dog barking and jumping playfully about the child.

They would have seen the boy scooping up handful after handful of water, throwing his arms high above his head, and the glittering droplets raining down upon them both in a celebration of laughter and life.

JOURNAL
Walking in Medjugorje 1991

Like most symbolic journeys, the path begins pleasantly enough. Through the village, out into the cultivation between cool vineyards, then beyond, the fields gently rising, dancing with summer flowers. The way narrows, hinting at what lies ahead. Now it climbs steeply and twists and turns among shady trees. Hawkers post themselves at natural resting points to sell votive candles.

The real pilgrims have set off long ago in the cool of the early morning. Some of them are already on the downward trek, weary and joyful. Ahead small groups are dotting the hillside. I'll pass the old and the slow ones, the barefoot pilgrims doing penance along the rocky path kneeling and praying at the stations of the cross.

For today, and I mean to make the most of this beautiful summer's day, I have taken my sun-glasses and a hat, protection from the Croatian sun. My shoulder bag contains a bottle of water, some bread and several oranges, a little money and a small hardback book of poems.

From the window of my whitewashed cell, I have been looking at these hills ever since arriving at the guest house here in Medjugorje, the huge horseshoe shaped ridge bearing the tiny cross on its summit and I've chosen today as the day to go walking.

For me the stations of the cross hold no significance, at least that's what I tell myself, merely resting places on the climb, to gaze across the expanding valley and the village becoming smaller and smaller as we wind upwards.

Since early morning, pilgrims have been trailing past the guest house in their hundreds, out towards the escarpment. There is no need to ask the way. As I set out, it is already hot. Gaining height, the hillside loses its garments of green and the steep sandy coloured hillside glitters with rock crystal.

It is very quiet on the hillside. Far away, below the rocky path, the little village of Medjugorje shimmers in the heat. Carried on the dry wind comes the sound of a bell tolling dolefully. I feel very detached yet very safe.

At length I reach the top and only now, at the foot of this concrete cross, does the enormity of the structure become clear. The plinth alone stands above head height. At its base the ground has been scooped away and in the dusty craters, hundreds upon hundreds of candles burn in the already intensely hot Croatian summer's day.

Ripples of heat dance horizontally and the air is filled with the fumes of burning tallow. Dozens of people standing silently, others approaching the pits with candle offerings walk into the searing furnace to place their lighted gifts upon a framework of metal stands. I watch for a while but am eager to leave this burning place and find an airy path.

Walking along the crest of the hillside like an ant might crawl along a garden path, I find there is nothing to follow. I simply have to concentrate on keeping to the ridge and staying upright. A gentle breeze replaces the sound of human voices and soon I am out of sight of the cross and following the ridge's gradual descent. Curiously there is a donkey, tethered to a boulder.

Quite abruptly the path drops steeply and there, about a hundred feet below me, is a small glade. A living gem of green, held in its glaring white stone setting. Almost at once I feel the sweet, cool updraft of the tiny verdant oasis. I clamber down rough chalky boulders, the flimsy leather weave of my sandals straining to contain my feet.

It is enclosed, the grass meadow is protected by thorny fortification. Here the boulders are chaotically piled, not stacked as before. Spiny brush has grown up between the rocks, creating a woody enclosure, beyond which I glimpse the sun filled meadow, a place that would in any story book, be enchanted. My legs and arms are bare but something compels me to gain entrance. Inching my way over and between the huge boulders, I reach the thorn barricade, then half turning, push against the springy scrub, almost wading as if in water, arms up around my head to keep from being grazed. My shirt catches, rips, tears free and I'm through, a little scratched, breathless on the edge of paradise.

After the hellish heat of the baked rocks this glade has the coolness of a cave, though sunlight is pouring onto every blade of grass and the green oasis shimmers and glints with light.

Wild flowers and grasses play host to darting winged insects and the air hums with the beating of their wings. The sound abruptly stops, seems to hold on a heartbeat as if my arrival has interfered with the cosmic play of things and there is deep, deep silence. I stand stock still on the edge and then the music of the insects' wings, like the toning of a singing bowl, resumes. Time passes.

Sitting in the glade, with the grass and flowers waving around my shoulders, and slipping into that rare moment of disconnection until my thoughts eject me, I become aware that I have been thinking about 'peace' and of course this cerebral act has broken the connection and once again I am on the outside looking in. Unqualified and unequipped, coming from the world of men and women as I do, to even think I can be a bringer of peace is silly and naïve. The best I could have hoped for has already happened, to have, for a few moments, been its guest. But now these thoughts like stones dropped into a pond, have made ripples and I come awake and realize it's time to go.

Once again I push through the ring of thorny bushes and suddenly, like a new-born, burst out onto the blinding white rock of the mountain. Opening my bag – it's strange I did not think to eat or drink whilst in the glade – I take out the water bottle, its branded label reminding me of supermarkets and shopping. The water is warm in the mouth and tastes lightly of plastic. I gulp and gulp realizing it's been too long to have gone without a drink. The oranges are lovely – warm and sweet with the bread. Looking about I see far below and to the east, the village of Medjugorje.

The next three and a half hours were spent in coming down off the mountain and what a gruelling walk. Every single step had to be negotiated, feet placed carefully on the tops of rounded boulders, judged, felt for, tested for slippage. Mostly I had to clamber down, or else slither over, the giant chalky marbles heaped one below the other.

Pretty soon I was exhausted because of the exertion, the heat and not having eaten enough or drunk enough and eventually landed on the back road at the base of the hillside, legs trembling so violently that I needed to lock my knees to keep from collapsing.

Somewhere, high on the slopes, I unwittingly walked into a large spider's mountain lair, triggering its signal line with my face. The animal had come scuttling down its thread in search of prey. I might have screamed aloud but all that escaped my throat was a strangled yelp.

The spider, sensing my size retreated back up its thread where it became invisible against the chalky white stone. Pulling backwards was my only means of escape and I felt the strand of spider silk snap, strong as a snagged stocking. I crouched on the hill, shuddering, and taking great care to give the creature a ridiculously wide berth, resumed my descent.

Climbing down the hillside, I'm telling myself the story, as if I'm already home and safe, victorious from the day's adventure. I stop to sit on my haunches and rest my legs, drink the remaining water and still my babbling mind. So hungry and exhausted was I from the exertion of the day, that I just about fell inside a tiny shop on the roadside, miles from anywhere and bought four bananas and ate them all as I walked.

I wonder about the sunglasses which I lost at some point during that day, a small twentieth century artefact, perhaps lodged in a crevice among the ancient rocks. I came away with two small pieces of pinkish rock crystal, picked up from the hillside earlier in the day. A strange exchange. They lie in all weathers outside on our kitchen window sill, just as my sunglasses do, somewhere on the hillside.

JOURNAL
Incident, Medjugorje 1991

Today I saw the dog. It's been two days since I and the American women carried him, bleeding, into a taxi. He's thinner and his ribs are showing. Even his coat has lost its lustre but he is alive. I wonder what he did and where he kept himself these two days. When I saw him today, it was evening again, about six o' clock.

A light breeze had come from the mountain, sweeping across the amphitheatre, swirling chalky dust around the chairs. I call the dog and he comes close, but not right up. The only thing in my bag is some dry bread and an orange, leftovers of the food taken on the walk. I offer him both the bread and the orange, talking softly to him, making my movements slow and deliberate. Possibly he knows I mean no harm but I guess he cannot afford to take the chance. So he stands a little way off, looking.

I place the orange on the stony ground and retreat to sit on one of the small white wooden chairs. He comes, sniffs, but doesn't take it. I do the same with the hunk of bread. He takes the bread and runs with it in his mouth a little way off where he buries it in the dry sandy earth. Maybe he's still too sick to eat. I put the rest of the bread down and he collects it and buries it too.

Flashback 1

The dog is quieter now. He lies there trembling slightly and from time to time he moves spasmodically. Someone has brought a little water and is slopping it over the dog's muzzle from cupped hands. Now blood tinges the wet marble floor.

The dog looks up from person to person. His eyes seem quizzical. Maybe he thinks he's dying – I do. I put both my hands on him, one over his head, the other on his shoulder. He's cold. I feel very helpless. In a moment of self-pity I think if I were dying I would like kind and gentle hands on me and that is why I touch him now. He is a handsome young dog, brown, sleek, well-muscled, grave dignified eyes. Someone is saying something. The dog gives a couple of desultory wags of his tail.

Flashback 2

The square in front of the church is crowded with pilgrims, sitting at wooden tables set under the trees and after the heat of the day, the evening air feels pleasant. The subdued, gentle murmur of hundreds of voices fills the space.

For some time now two dogs have been playing a sort of tag game, jawing and pawing at each other. Without realizing it, they occupy centre stage. The air is warm, the square filled with evening sunlight when silently, swift as an assassin, a stocky young man with wild curly black hair and beard steps in. The wind billows his immaculate cream coloured shirt and fills it full like a sail.

Flashback 3

Suddenly, in his raised hand there is a cudgel. He smashes it downwards on the unsuspecting dogs. A hideous canine scream. One of the dogs drops like a stone and the other, a black dog, leaps away and is gone.

The cudgel falls again and even again on the howling creature. And then abruptly, the man has gone, turned away, simply striding away to leave the air rent with the screams of the dog.

His hind legs have collapsed, the front ones desperately paddle on the smooth marble. In unison the crowd gives a groan. The spectacle of the scrabbling dog is unbearable, one moment so skilfully playing, now spinning round and round in injured panic.

Flashback 4

I feel my legs jerk me to a standing position and I'm moving forward and at the same time thinking *oh god, don't let me be the one to get there first* but no one else is moving. I reach the animal, wondering if it will bite, and putting my arms around its upper body, the back legs are sprawled and useless, bear him to the ground with my chest.

Strangely detached, I hear myself saying *lie still, lie still.* I hold him there. Now people are all around. Shock. The dog goes silent. Motionless.

As the minutes pass the crowd thins. It becomes dusk. The dog is still breathing. Now there's only half a dozen of us around him. The American woman declares she'll take him back to her hotel, then adds she wants someone to come with her – no wait - she says - it's better if two people come because after she's gotten the dog to her hotel, the other two are gonna see each other back to town.

Flashback 5

At the taxi rank the driver shrugs indifferently. We climb into the taxi. Three strangers with the inert dog. Later in the taxi, in silence with my companion, we lurch back to town along the pot-holed road. On the beat up seating I see blood on the upholstery, a small smudge, colourless in the orange street light, but still wet and glistening.

I let my companion pay, she's dollars richer than me and since she offers I don't make a fuss. Once more at the church square, empty and dark, we face each other, strangers temporarily united, both of us silently weeping now at the moment of parting, and wordlessly, we embrace.

Then turning away I take the narrow tarmac road that winds between the vineyards, back to the guest house, walking under the night sky.

SKY BIRD

Long, long ago, when the earth was young, it was always summer. Under the warm sun, fragrant blossoms of orange and red covered the land. At night, flowers of blue, violet and purple, the colour of the void, opened their petals when the moon and stars shone in the sky.

Grasses the colour of jade and emerald, swayed across the hillsides and plains like a lazy green sea. Ripe fruits and nuts hung in clusters from laden branches of the trees ready to bow down to outstretched hands.

The inhabitants of the earth were happy and content because there was always plenty to eat.

A huge forest covered half the earth, giving shade to all who dwelt under its vast green canopy.

Among its creatures lived Sky Bird. She was vain and deceitful. She strutted and preened and fluffed her feathers, of which she was especially proud.

Sometimes her plumage was tinted with colours of the sky, sometimes they glowed with soft earth colours or were stained the colour of the sea. But even though Sky Bird was probably the most beautiful of all the birds in the Great Forest, she was an unpopular inhabitant, for she was a thief.

Nothing was safe from the glittering eye of Sky Bird and nothing could satisfy her greed. She stole shiny pebbles and pastel shells from the fishes on the river bed, soft mosses from the nests of other birds, and acorns and nuts from the squirrels. Soon the nest of Sky Bird was overflowing but Sky Bird was not content.

One day she decided to leave the greenwood and fly up to The Great Dome, home of the Sky Queen, where she had heard, was all manner of treasure.

She flew, and she flew and she flew, higher and higher until at last she reached The Great Dome. Sky Bird was dazzled by all that she saw and her heart grew hungry.

The Sky Queen's palace was built of crystal, gold and silver and decorated with ruby, amethyst, topaz, emerald and lapis. It shimmered and sparkled with light and Sky Bird was overcome with a terrible longing.

Night after night Sky Bird returned to The Great Dome and under the cloak of darkness, she stole from the Sky Queen, always returning to her nest by daybreak.

Quite soon Sky Bird's huge nest was filled with stolen treasure. The animals were displeased with Sky Bird whom they felt would surely bring disgrace and punishment upon them all and so they held council at the foot of the old oak. Eventually it was decided that Sky Bird would go to The Great Dome and ask the Sky Queen for forgiveness but Sky Bird refused to go because she was afraid and she flew away deep into the forest and hid.

The Sky Queen was furious when she heard what had happened and she shook with a cold rage, vexed that one of her subjects should show such ungratefulness by stealing from her, for it was she, Sky Queen who had created a wonderland on earth for all to enjoy. She had made the sun to shine all year long, for rain to fall and fill the springs and streams, flowers to bloom and fruits to ripen.

Angrily Sky Queen strode back and forth through her palace and her flowing robes caused an icy wind to sweep across the Great Forest far below. It withered every leaf upon every tree and soon the floor of the forest was covered in a carpet of dead leaves.

Now the bare branches of the Great Forest were exposed to the gaze of the Sky Queen. She looked down and saw Sky Bird's nest in the heart of a giant elm tree at the centre of the forest. It was full of the Sky Queen's jewels. In fury the Sky Queen flung the jewels across the face of the earth, then she summoned Sky Bird. 'You have taken what is not yours' she said.

Sky Bird trembled and wept. 'Forgive me great Sky Queen for I have been greedy and betrayed your trust.'

'This is so' said the Sky Queen. 'Now listen to me Sky Bird. This is how you shall make amends.'

She commanded Sky Bird to remove her lovely plumage. The iridescent feathers of blue and emerald green, and her lovely night feathers of indigo and pearl.

So too Sky Bird was stripped of her bold scarlet and crimson feathers that flashed in the sun and instead, Sky Bird was made to put on a feathered coat of austere black and white. How poor Sky Bird wept.

Finally, the Sky Queen took away Sky Bird's name, and she became known as Magpie, which means thieving bird.

Ever since that time the Sky Queen has sent cold winds to make the leaves fall from the trees and this we have learnt to call Autumn.

It is then that Magpie goes in search of the Sky Queen's jewels wherever they lay, scattered over the earth. When she finds one, she must make the long journey back to the Sky Queen's palace, carrying the jewel in her beak. Should Magpie fail to find a jewel, the Sky Queen will not allow the summer to return and everyone living on the earth shall perish.

So far, Magpie has not failed in her task though she finds the work harder with the passing of the years.

So today, if you see a magpie in her black and white dress you may be minded of a time of eternal summer. Spare her a kindness as she goes about her business and know that this is why magpies are always on the lookout for shiny things.

THE EMPTY WINDOW

She had come up to London to see a new exhibition. At the gallery she eagerly rushed the three flights of stairs, too impatient to wait for the lift, the expensive catalogue clamped firmly under her arm.

On entering gallery thirteen, the heavy plate glass door swung closed behind her, distant sounds of the busy street with its noisy traffic, abruptly blotted out.

The silence crept in around her, a brooding expectancy hung in the air as if the room was waiting. In the small private gallery, the lighting had been dimmed so as not to fade the pen and ink sketches that hung, equally spaced, along the wood lined walls.

The silence expanded. Taking a deep breath she slowly exhaled and began to examine the finely drawn sketches, referring to the catalogue each time she moved to another frame. Finally she came to the last picture in the long gallery.

It was a bleak landscape with a house set in the middle distance. Derelict and dilapidated, the house stood on uneven ground, strangely out of kilter, and it carried an air of dark foreboding.

The nightmarish front door was a gaping black space, broken shutters hung from the crumbling walls. All the windows were boarded up, save for a small crooked one, right at the top of the house, in the attic under the eaves. A single, dusty, window pane against a dark interior.

The catalogue informed her that this picture was entitled, "The Empty Window".

The woman took a step closer, then another and then, one more.

At closing time the gallery shut its ornate front doors and a small contingent of cleaners came in through a side entrance. In the dimly lit space that was gallery thirteen, the cleaner went about his nightly routine, stopping to pick up a catalogue where it lay fallen. He dropped it into the black sack on his cleaning trolley, without glancing at the picture of the helter-skelter house, with its small crooked window, where a woman's face was pressed close against the glass, her mouth open in a long, silent scream.

THE GIRL WHO GAVE EVERYTHING AWAY

There was a little girl who was very nice and so, not surprisingly, people liked her. How did people show that they liked her? Well, one way was to tell her what a nice person she was. Another way was if her friends might buy her presents or give her useful things.

But the little girl didn't know how to hold on to things and so every time someone would say to her, 'Oh, how nice, I see you have a new pencil case, give it to me' – she would!

So on Monday the little girl's mother gave her a new pair of red woollen gloves to keep her hands warm because it was getting cold. When she got to school some of her friends said how lovely the gloves were and another person said, 'I want your gloves. Give them to me'.

And so she did.

When it was time to go home after school, it had become very cold and our little girl in the story had given away her lovely red woollen gloves and so her hands got very cold as she walked home through the snow and she started to cry because of the pain in her fingers.

On Tuesday her father gave her a beautiful story book and that afternoon when the little girl was with all her friends, someone said to her, 'What a nice story book, I wish I had a book like that, why don't you give it to me?'

So the little girl gave her story book away.

When she got home, her father said 'Where is the story book I gave to you this morning, I would like you to read to me'.

But the little girl had given the book away and she turned her eyes to the floor and said to her father, 'Father I gave the book away, so I can't read to you'.

And she felt sad.

On Wednesday her sisters, because they loved her, gave the little girl a skipping rope. They knew how much she liked to skip in the playground.

When the little girl got to school some children said 'We like your skipping rope, if you give us the skipping rope, we will be your friends and let you play with us'.

So the little girl gave away her skipping rope, but the children were naughty and they broke their promise and they wouldn't let her join in their games. They took the skipping rope and ran away and the little girl started to cry.

On Thursday her Aunt came to visit and gave the little girl a beautiful shawl. It was so beautiful and it must have cost a lot of money.

'Oh how lovely' said the little girl and she put the shawl on and ran out of the house to go and show her friends.

But some of her friends were jealous and they didn't want the little girl to keep the shawl, so they made a horrid plan and this is what they did.

'Little girl, your shawl makes you look ugly, why don't you sell it to us? We'll give you fifty pence for your shawl'.

And the little girl sold her beautiful shawl and the children ran away laughing.

On the way home the little girl thought to herself, now I will go and buy myself some chocolate but on the way she dropped the money and could not find it anywhere and so she had no shawl and even worse, no chocolate!

On Friday the little girl woke up in the morning but she felt sad. Why? Well, let us ask the little girl for ourselves.

'Little girl, why are you feeling so sad this morning?'

The little girl dries her eyes and says, 'Because on Monday my mother gave me a pair of red woollen gloves and I gave them away and now my hands are cold.

On Tuesday my father gave me a story book and I gave the book away and now I can't read to him.

On Wednesday my sisters gave me a skipping rope and I gave the rope away and now I can't play with my friends.

On Thursday my Aunt gave me a beautiful shawl but some people told me it was ugly and so I sold it and then I lost my money.

Today it is Friday and I have nothing. That is why I am sad.'

Then her mother, her father, all her sisters and her aunt saw how she must be feeling and they said one by one 'Little girl, the presents we give you are to show you how special you are but if you give them away every time, you will forget that you are so special.

Keep them for yourself so that every time you look at your presents you will remember how nice you are and how much we all love you.'

We will never know who the little girl was, because she had also given away her name, but her grandmother, who is a wise and good woman, and who loves the little girl very much indeed, knows what the little girl has done, and has kept her name in a safe and secret place because grandmother knows that one day, our little girl will want to get her name back.

Part 2
& Verse

ALCHEMY

Father, mother,
sister, brother,
friend and mentor,
alchemist.

Always constant,
guide and witness,
inspiration,
I am blessed.

ASCENSION

Brothers and sisters,
you lift me high,
where my feet find purchase
upon narrow ledges
on the rocks of self-discovery.

Then, shall I not reach out and
elevate you higher still?
For this is not a solitary struggle,
but the Ascension of humankind.

And strung with ropes of love,
we shall attain the summits
of our jewelled peaks.

BEFORE DUSK

Before dusk rushed us from the hill, I built a fire
from fallen branches, grey flecked and brittle,
gathered from the dry ditch
running beside the row of ancient trees.

Before dusk came to lie across the high meadows
and smudge the golden grasses with inky stain,
I carried bundles of sinuous branches
and bore them, like sleeping children, in my arms.

Before dusk crept out on three sides,
I built an ancient henge
from broad, flat stones, lugged from the stream bed,
to trap the fire and stop it running with the wind.

Before dusk, as the sun dipped towards the land,
a spirited breeze sprang from down the valley
and came racing through the camp,
pummelling and tugging at the tents.

In the rapid moments before dusk and darkness,
the crimson sun slid between the sky and ancient land,
pulling down the last of the brightness,

And from a distant memory, still smouldering in the brain,
I lit our campsite fire and watched its orange heart
as it beat about the hearth stones, shedding light
into another night.

BY NOW

You were stored away,
down in the cool, dark earth
around the sapling's inquisitive roots.
Your cremated bones,
granular to the touch,
lay gleaming
against the dark soil.
By now you are part of the tree.

All winter long
the sapling withstood storm and pale frost,
while, in the quiet ground
the alchemical marriage began -
your mineral energy coursed up
through the heartwood
into leaf and shoot,
drinking rain and reaching for the light.
By now you are part of the sun.

The following spring,
held aloft on juvenile stems
and wearing pink blossom,
you danced for the blue sky,
then fell like bridal petals
back to earth.
By now you are one with the seasons.

Now, you are the heat
of crackling firewood
burning hot in the stove,
wreathed in white smoke
and gently rising
into a dark sky.
By now you are one with the air.

Later, from the silent grate,
I carry your powdery remains
into the winter garden,
and lay them
at the foot of the tree's broad trunk,
ash bright
against the dark soil.
By now you are part of the whole.

CIRCLE OF TIME

Somewhere in the circle of time
there is a land through which a golden river flows.
Silence pulsates in perfect harmony,
harmony vibrates in perfect pitch.
The air is pure and sweet like nectar,
radiance floods the land.
For every day, a lotus blooms,
a floral generation borne upon the waters.
Softly glides the river
through the Golden Gates of Perfection . . . .

On and on,

Across the fertile plain of Eden
runs the quickening silver ribbon and towards evening
a risen argent moon is twinned upon its surface.
Soft night falls and she lays
her blue-black cloak upon the river's sinuous form
as it twists and turns toward a lesser kingdom,
to fall in broad sheets of silver
over the cataract of time.

Darkness.

In a middle eastern sky
a burnished copper sun pierces the blue.
By the light of love alone a child is born
though the spark is not human,
and when the child becomes a man, he calls himself

The Light of the World.
So in a parody of worship, an insane, profane joke
I hang him high upon a cross to light the way.
Yet his message of Love still flickers and flares
across the chasm of ignorance
to the farther shores of separation.

Now . . .

Beside the river running rust red
we labour under the yoke of lust,
and momentarily free we cry out,
though we have forgotten
the name of the Beloved.

Yet within this space, this place, this time,
here at the mighty confluence where the waters foam and froth,
weighed down with iron ballast, we plumb the depths of experience,
and under crushing atmospheres of pressure
sometimes a diamond is revealed.
Deep in its multifaceted heart we glimpse
Eternal Truth.
A jewelled fortune within reach. It has lain beneath the silt of time
waiting, waiting to be remembered.
Now you have it in your grasp – hold fast!
And *remember* . . .

Somewhere in the circle of time
There is a land through which a golden river flows.

ECHOES

I sing to the hills and mountains,
valleys flood with the sound of my calling,
shadows move, the grass blows.

Across vast distances
echoes of my longing come back to me -
should I answer?

FOWL AND THE PUSSYCAT

Fowl and the pussycat went to see
A beautiful pea-green boat.
They took some honey and plenty of money
In the form of a large wad of notes.
The fowl surveyed the boat in its yard,
He surveyed it from near and from far –
Then said,
"Oh Pussy, oh Pussy, oh Pussy my love,
Couldn't we buy a car?"

GIFTS

These objects, these gifts,
occupying space and memory,
where time is flowing past them
and through them.

Here, their flattened forms
of colour and graphite laid upon paper.
In another place,
solid reality.

Intrinsically themselves,
they stand for something else.

And elsewhere that is no place,
the thoughts,
that brought
these gifts
to me.

HERALDRY

She is a war torn flag
fluttering in life's breeze.
Purple, blue, gold and red,
crimson for the blood she's shed.

Loudly cracks the cloth of history,
a ragged semaphore for mystery.
lament or joyous testament?

She's shredding, fraying strand by strand,
at last unravelling in the wind
she'll stand,
revealed, reconciled,
healed.

MARINE DRIVE (OR BLOOD MONEY)

We sit uncomfortably
in my sister's car
on hot asphalt
caught in lines of taxis and motor scooters.

For the beggars,
traffic lights are temporary snares
in which we are caught,
catatonic with uneasy conscience.

The leprous youth approaches,
I twitch and struggle in the trap
tearing my mind on its rusty jaws . . . .

The lights change to green.
Green for flight, and I
drop
a bloodied   coin
into
his tattered hand.

SENTINEL

Keeping watch in full moonlight,
shadows slide across
the silent valley.

Small orange fire
in ring of hearth stone
cannot push away the darkness,

Nor my hand arrest
the silent blade
that enters the heart and stills it.

THE OCEAN

Her body,
usually so co-operative,
conspires
with ego
to silence her.

While her true self
struggles to articulate the words
that are its passport to inner
freedom,
battalions of peptides are released,
triggered by crackling, flashing synapses,
urgent
with their messages of danger.

Her tongue,
normally so fluid
with its torrent of words,
sticks to the palate glued firmly by
fear,
but you are witness;
she cannot say it did not happen.

Her message,
sealed in a bottle
and cast into the cosmic ocean was
carried on sound-waves
to another shore, to be
opened
by the hand of the Unseen.

WHILE HEADS LIE SLEEPING

While heads lie sleeping
or not sleeping,
I rise and dress and step into a new day.

On the other side of an urban wall
lies nature.
Unfettered by bricks and mortar,
she stretches gracefully along still water
mirrors herself on its surface.
She has nothing to hide, she is beautiful.

Now, I will go in search
of that place of beauty within,
where a child's feet has made small pathways
through green glades and along grassy banks.
I have not yet glimpsed the child
but I know she is there,
I saw her footprints in the dew.

WHILST WE ARE FRIENDS

When we were tillers what did we sow
In golden fields and shady groves?
When we were travellers where did we roam?
Along the dusty roads.
Whilst we are friends what shall we exchange?
Happiness, joy and love.

When we were lovers, what made us remember
The glittering jewel that lay in the embers?
When we were seekers what did we discover?
That I am your sister and you are my brother.
Whilst we are friends what shall we exchange?
Happiness, joy and love.

When we were poets, what did we say
When the heart was overflowing?
Now we are children what shall we play
Among sweet flowers growing?
Whilst we are friends what shall we exchange?
Happiness, joy and love.

WINGS

You were the Blackbird who woke me,
the wise Hoopoe that spoke
of a distant State of Mind.
You were the migrant Swift who
persuaded me to take flight.

If you were these then,
might you not also be a Skylark
climbing into the blue and gold,
and the fabulous Phoenix
rising from the ashes of your past?

I wish you wings.

ZODIAC

Three times in her life, illness gripped her by her sex,
laying her low and so developed a cautious view
of pleasure,
the sting in the tail – the pun is intentional.

Like a beaten cur, nursing its wounds,
her thoughts became heavy – swollen and throbbing with
unspent energy.

Encased in a thermal shell of ice-olation,
desire crawled like molten lava, leaving in its wake a trail
of glittering magma.

Fresh winds blew her to a southern coast where
warm waters lapped her feet. For a time she swam
happily with the fishes.

Then, searching for something beyond her watery habitat,
one day leaped high in a silvery arc and lay gasping
on the rocks.

There, in a scorpion's embrace
under waxing moons, they danced the intimate steps
of self-knowing.

Now from across the zodiac he comes on cloven hooves,
smelling of sweet moist earth and meadow flowers, and she,
like a seed,

Containing the knowledge of things to come,
and sensing the promise of rain
splits open.

MEDITATIONS – *a series of short poems*

The fire
briefly took my hand in playfulness –
yet I feel it still.

Here's the driving rain
swelling the door in its frame –
it's stuck 'til springtime.

When does it become marriage –
this scented courtship
of rain and red earth?

Tasting infinity
in every snowflake –
like kissing your lips.

Mountains to marbles,
the ocean pounds the shoreline –
how many lifetimes?

Time himself slows down
to pause and glimpse the snowflakes
sinking to the ground.

Light speeds everywhere
flirting with time –
whereas love is a constant.

On long sleepless nights
I drift in my bed upon
an underground stream.

I was up for it at first light –
but by tea-time
I wasn't so sure!

Nature expresses herself best
in youthfulness –
before time scars us.

It looked so pretty,
so I tried it on for size –
this shroud they call life.

Recalling fondly
the tinkling of silver spoons
upon summer cups.

When the lake tired of our nocturnal offering,
it bade us goodnight.

Autumn –
the low hills stubbornly wearing
their pale grey raincoats.

Rains have washed the air –
the valley floats
decanted in a crystal bowl.

Pale wood-smoke serpent,
coiling from its glowing nest,
tastes the wintry air.

Scavenging for wood –
twigs snapping underfoot
like fire in the grate.

The sun it rises,
there's all that stuff in between –
then it sets again.

Ignited by sun –
fierce fire-rainbow
raged across sky tundra.

A shriek in the blue,
dark shape, the other silver –
two buzzards playing.

Autumn mist, chill wind
etch their messages –
leaves fall like unread letters.

Majestic forest!
I have slept in your great rooms
under burning stars.

you and me are names
called out in separateness –
'til Thou and I are one.

Suddenly comes joy –
how swift these fleet emotions –
what next, I wonder?

How do I reach You,
hear You, walk alongside You?
all these with the Heart.

Every day
it's a'gettin' closer,
comin' faster than you think!

Being so in love,
I throw my arms wide open
to the formless One.

First thing to be done
on grey winter evenings –
light the fire.

Here's the rain that falls in sheets for days on end –
greening the hillside.

Here's the rainbow straddling the vale and village –
child of mist and sun.

Here are the swallows
describing in arcs and planes, simple existence.

Cradle me in moss
when the air is soft and close –
wrap me in your roots.

Spring's green shoots unpick
winter's iron manacle –
then how she dances!

The ocean receives
into its swelling bosom
her sons and daughters.

Along the earthwork
lofty trees toppled –
cooling moonbeams bathe the wounds.

Sculptor of the heart,
Mason of the mind,
fashion me in Your image.

Arrows splinter on my breast,
coals are quenched
beneath my tireless feet.

Oh son of Bharat!
I am the taste in water,
the heat in fire.

Fragile container
of stardust and love
that I, for now, inhabit.

When it's time
to leave this warm cave of blood and bone,
who will point the way?

Exquisite screen
of cloud and leafy filigree
veils the silver Queen.

Red fox
picking her way
through winter snowdrops.

Fearless warrior –
robed in mist, bright blade of frost,
turns to face the day.

.

Hush –
snow has come to lie beside
the sleeping flowers of the wood.

Walking through the wood –
my footsteps creaking
over freshly fallen snow.

When did we decide
to smother you in concrete
beautiful Mother?

Knowing there is You,
what fell sorrow
could pierce the breastplate of joy?

Astound me with Light,
bombard me with Miracles,
furnish me with Love.

Not daring to knock -
Your voice from within, laughing
'but this is your home!'

Sometimes a thought,
more lucid than sunshine,
carries me back to your eyes.

Who *were* those *people*
around your bedside mother –
before you left us?

Distilled from darkness –
fragrant rose-petal bowl
holds one drop of starlight.

Pawing at the fish –
unperturbed they glide,
deeper than a cat may wish.

Pale, powdery moth
flitting, fluttering, whirring –
dusted by moonbeams.

Pale white galleon
sails anew each evening –
dropping anchor at dawn.

Jealous solar King
cannot chase pale lunar Queen
from his airy sky.

Soft breeze stirs the lake –
then granite mountain
turns to rippling watered silk.

Ascending skylarks
loose their musical torrent
from a pale blue sky.

You have a place more spacious
than any landscape –
you know it as Mind.

Hang up your costumes!
there's nothing more to do now
but sleep the long sleep.

Walking on air
is a great deal easier
than walking on water.

Time –
do you weigh it, measure it, then watch it fly
or try and save it?

What should take their place –
if sun and moon did battle
'cross the starry waste?

Circles spread outwards
as the watchful heron's beak
breaks the still water.

Rushing of snow melt,
foaming from the mountain-side,
brims the agate pool.

Mirrored in the lake –
skein of flying geese aloft,
shoal of fish beneath.

Under the rock pool –
speckled trout unblinking
bathes in dappled sunlight.

Deadly semaphore –
buzzard and pigeon
flapping madly.

Pockets of warm air -
ambling down the leafy lane
my hand in yours.

Seven subtle hues
in sky of battleship grey –
fading in sunlight.

When words must finish
use the language of the heart –
then words are finished.

All of creation
awaits mankind's ascension
to a brave new world.

When the heart is full
then love and love
'til the vessel be empty.

Exploding giant,
tracked across millennia –
your light streaks outwards.

Birth of the cosmos –
whose life and death is written
in light upon dark.

Anchored in blue sky,
hanging over patchwork fields –
a fleet of cloud-ships.

Crouched in a dust bowl
and warmed by afternoon sun –
small tabby she-cat.

Spaced between the spokes
of my winding garden path –
yellow tulips stand.

Under iron skies
of battleship grey –
tender snowdrops ranked.

Poor small garden frog –
his terracotta palace
broken by the ice.

Rain waters Earth –
then wind to dry and sun to warm her
as she dances.

Summer heat, some rain –
and the ancient damson tree
ruby julep makes.

After the storm,
torn from the branch –
my wind chime smashed upon the wet earth.

Comet pebble flung
through space
to skim the surface of earth's atmosphere.

Trying to reach You –
my thoughts wing upwards
and graze the edge of heaven.

Black holes in space-time
draw light into the centre –
and history stops.

Ask the Beloved –
shall I come to you naked,
or veiled and disguised?

Stars whirl in night sky –
churning heaven's inky dark
to a brightening dawn.

Robin sits atop my garden spade
as if to say
don't stop, keep digging!

Land and lake alike,
locked in winter's iron embrace –
slumbering 'til spring.

Scent of wild garlic
rising from the damp spring earth –
a carpet of spice.

In forgetfulness
each morning new,
I blunder through the spider's silk.

He's still a puppy
mouthing everything he can –
time to grow up soon.

Owl hoots –
frisbee gliding
straight to its mark.

Holly-berry, mistletoe,
through the solstice gate we go –
winter's offering.

Transcendent wisdom –
filtered by neural net
to chalice of the heart.

The fragment of five -
then seven staccato beats
to capture the phrase.

Crescent moon hanging
pregnant with her dark daughter,
full twenty-eight days.

Not everyone
stops
at the fountain of wisdom –
drink deeply pilgrim.

Last night the stars
were within touching distance
when the world wobbled past.

A mundane meeting
on ordinary business –
the eyes know better.

Remember me Lord –
for I left so long ago.

A gap in the hedge –
trying to see
what might have been.

Old ones
young ones
time is the sniper.

If time heals everything,
What need of surgeons?

Frog,
how did you find this tiny ornamental pool –
did you scent it?

On blustery nights
the wind booms down the chimney –
he's all bluff I think.

Tall slender grasses
rolling like a golden sea –
blown by summer wind.

Orange and amber fire-fall
Streaming upwards
to fill the sky pool.

Within an acorn,
in the tiniest chamber –
the sylvan blueprint.

Wandering through
neglected websites -
back to the home page.